I Can Feel Better Now!

T0142670

Anxiety Release

LOU L. HOLLAND

Copyright © 2020 Lou L. Holland.

All rights reserved. No part of this book may be used or reproduced by any means, graphic, electronic, or mechanical, including photocopying, recording, taping or by any information storage retrieval system without the written permission of the author except in the case of brief quotations embodied in critical articles and reviews.

Balboa Press books may be ordered through booksellers or by contacting:

Balboa Press
A Division of Hay House
1663 Liberty Drive
Bloomington, IN 47403
www.balboapress.com
1 (877) 407-4847

Because of the dynamic nature of the Internet, any web addresses or links contained in this book may have changed since publication and may no longer be valid. The views expressed in this work are solely those of the author and do not necessarily reflect the views of the publisher, and the publisher hereby disclaims any responsibility for them.

Any people depicted in stock imagery provided by Getty Images are models, and such images are being used for illustrative purposes only.
Certain stock imagery © Getty Images.

ISBN: 978-1-9822-4497-2 (sc)
ISBN: 978-1-9822-4496-5 (e)

Print information available on the last page.

Balboa Press rev. date: 04/01/2020

BALBOA.PRESS
A DIVISION OF HAY HOUSE

I Can Feel Better Now!

Anxiety Release

Book 1 of the, 'Some of my Favourite People' collection

Hello, my name is Oliver, and lately I've been feeling some feelings that I've never felt before.

Sometimes I feel scared and I don't know why. I feel nervous almost all of the time and sometimes my chest starts to hurt and I start to breathe really fast! Sometimes my head hurts and sometimes my tummy hurts so much that I have to stay home from school. Sometimes I just want to stay in my room and hide away from everyone..

Someone told me that the way I've been feeling is called anxiety. But all I know is that it doesn't feel good, it feels really scary.

I have a friend named Annie, and she is one of my very favourite people. Her nickname is Annie Banannie, but I like to call her Banana. This nickname suits her because Annie makes me feel like the color yellow. She feels like the sun. When she is around I always feel better. Banana is warm and bright and she makes me feel safe. She is happy almost all of the time! I asked her how she can always be so happy and why she doesn't feel scared like I do, and do you know what she told me?

Banana told me that she tries to always think happy thoughts. She says that if something doesn't feel good when she thinks about it, then she just doesn't think about it anymore. She picks a happy thought instead. Annie says that if we think about things that feel good, then we will start to feel good too!

Do you know what that means?

That means that we can start feeling better right now!

Who are some people that make you feel warm & safe?

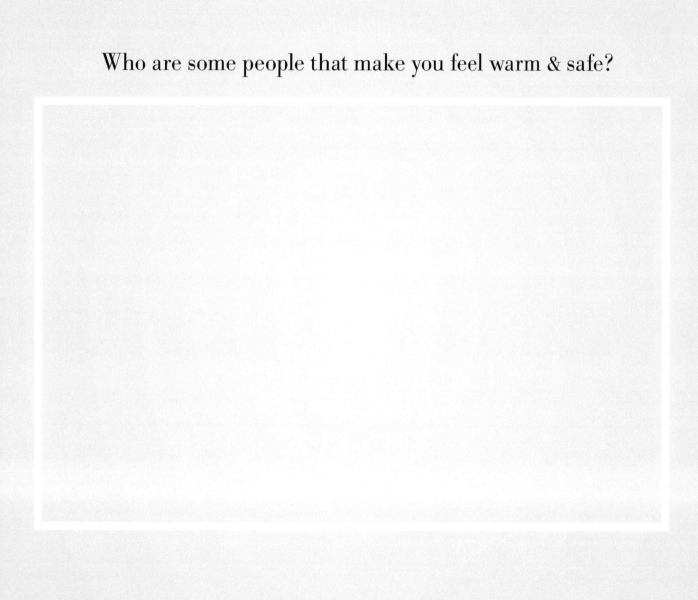

Some of the things Annie likes to think about is the sun shining on her face, playing with worms, swinging on her favourite swing at the park and climbing her favourite tree. Do you know what her very favourite thing to daydream about is? It's candy!

Annie loves candy so much, that she imagines that she lives in a house made of candies and sweet, yummy treats…What are some things you like to daydream about?

My very favourite thing to daydream about

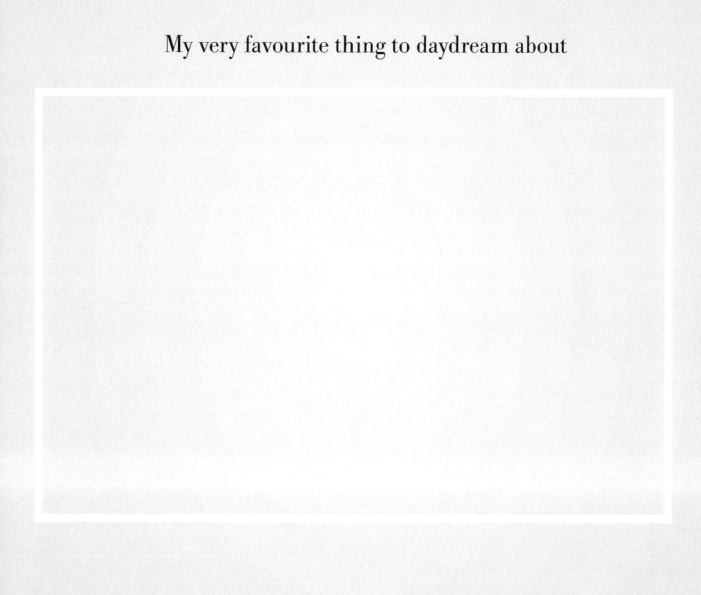

Annie says that she feels safe when she thinks happy thoughts, so she really likes to think them! When she starts to feel funny in her tummy, or if she gets scared to go to school, or when she starts to worry about scary things happening, she makes herself think about something else instead. Banana says you can think about anything you want, but you just have to make sure it feels good when you think it!

When you start to feel scared, what are some things you could think about instead? What do your happy thoughts look like?

Maybe you could write them down or draw a picture of them.

My Happy Thoughts

Maybe you have a happy memory that you like thinking about?

My Favourite Memories

Annie told me that sometimes she worries about her mom and dad, and that sometimes she doesn't get along with her brother and sister. Sometimes the kids at school tease her and then she comes home in a grumpy mood. When this happens, my good friend Banana likes to hang upside down on her bed until she starts to giggle. She stops thinking about the kids at school and she starts thinking about her favourite camping trip instead. The one where her and her cousin built a fort in the trees.

It doesn't take her long until she feels happy again!

Things that make me feel better

So remember, if it doesn't feel good when you think about it, just find something that does!

Annie's mom says that when Annie decides to feel good, instead of bad, and when

Annie decides to pick happy thoughts instead of scary ones, that she is invincible!

Invincible means powerful.

Her mom says that we can all feel safe and powerful anytime we want, but we've got to pick good thoughts to think!

Do you know which good feeling thoughts you are going to think about next time you feel scared? Which thoughts will make you feel invincible?

Annie Banannie is super smart. Do you see why she is one of my favourite people? I like her being my friend, she really knows how to help me feel better!

Tomorrow I am going to practice thinking happy thoughts all day long. Maybe you can find an adult to practice with you? Then you can both feel better! It will be a great day!

Now close your eyes and think of something that
makes you happy, and think about it a lot!

See? You really can feel better now!

Printed in the United States
By Bookmasters